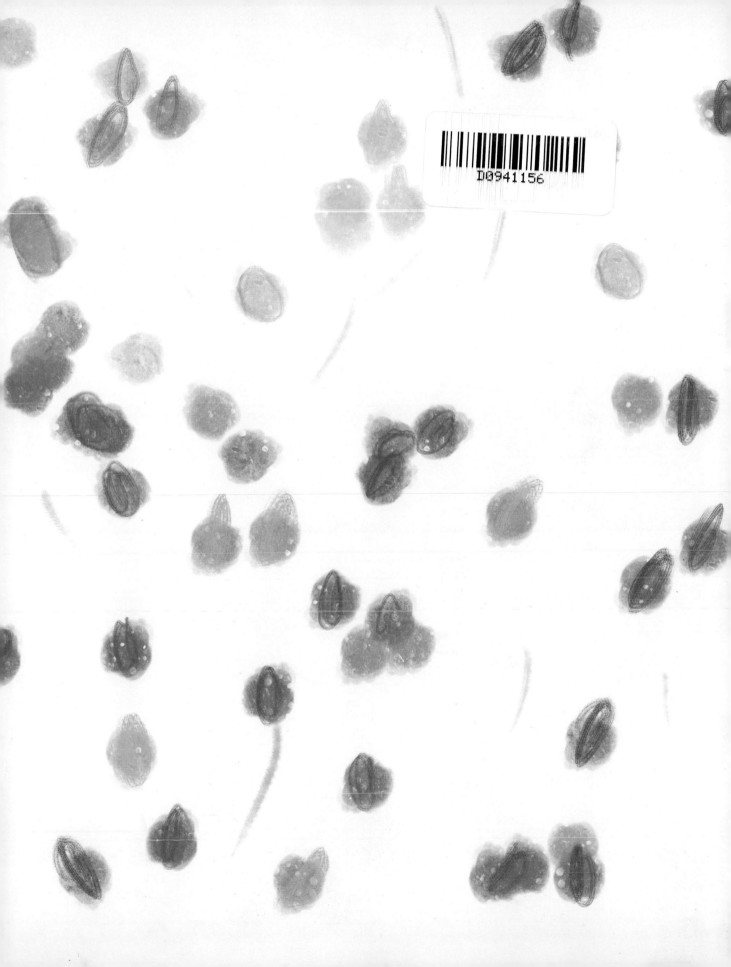

D0941156

Emma's Sunflower

By Phillipa Warden

Illustrated by
Grace Ward

Purple Butterfly Press
An Imprint of Kat Biggie Press
Columbia, SC

Emma's Sunflower

Copyright ©2022 by Phillipa Warden

All rights reserved. No part of this book may be reproduced, stored in a retrieval system, or transmitted in any form or by any means, electronic, electrostatic, magnetic tape, mechanical, photocopying, recording or otherwise, without the written permission of the publishers.

Illustrations by Grace Ward
Editor Caroline Smith
Design by Sunny Duran

Published by: Purple Butterfly Press

Publisher's Cataloging-In-Publication Data
(Prepared by The Donohue Group, Inc.)

Names: Warden, Phillipa, author. | Ward, Grace, illustrator.
Title: Emma's sunflower / written by Phillipa Warden ; illustrated by Grace Ward.
Description: Columbia, SC : Purple Butterfly Press, an imprint of Kat Biggie Press, [2022] | Interest age level: 003-005. | Summary: "Mother Nature has a cunning plan and, much to Emma's delight, a discarded sunflower seed snuggled deep in the soil grows through the different seasons and emerges on her birthday"--Provided by publisher.
Identifiers: ISBN 9781955119238 (hardback) | ISBN 9781955119139 (paperback) | ISBN 9781955119146 (ebook)
Subjects: LCSH: Girls--Juvenile fiction. | Sunflowers--Juvenile fiction. | Greenfinch--Juvenile fiction. | CYAC: Girls--Fiction. | Sunflowers--Fiction. | Birds--Fiction.
Classification: LCC PZ7.1.W3687 Em 2022 (print) | LCC PZ7.1.W3687 (ebook) | DDC [E]--dc23

For Emma and her
little brother
Rupert

It was Autumn. Bronzed
leaves danced playfully
to the ground beneath
the apple tree.
A bird feeder swayed in
a gust of wind and a
family of greenfinches
jostled to feed at the
sunflower seeds that
Emma had packed
into it.

Emma watched   from her window,
delighted by   the happy scene.

Emma loved the birds
pale cloudy greys,

olive greens, and
sunny yellows.

One of the birds had a
lightning bolt on its back,
so Emma named him Flash.

A large black crow

Emma's house

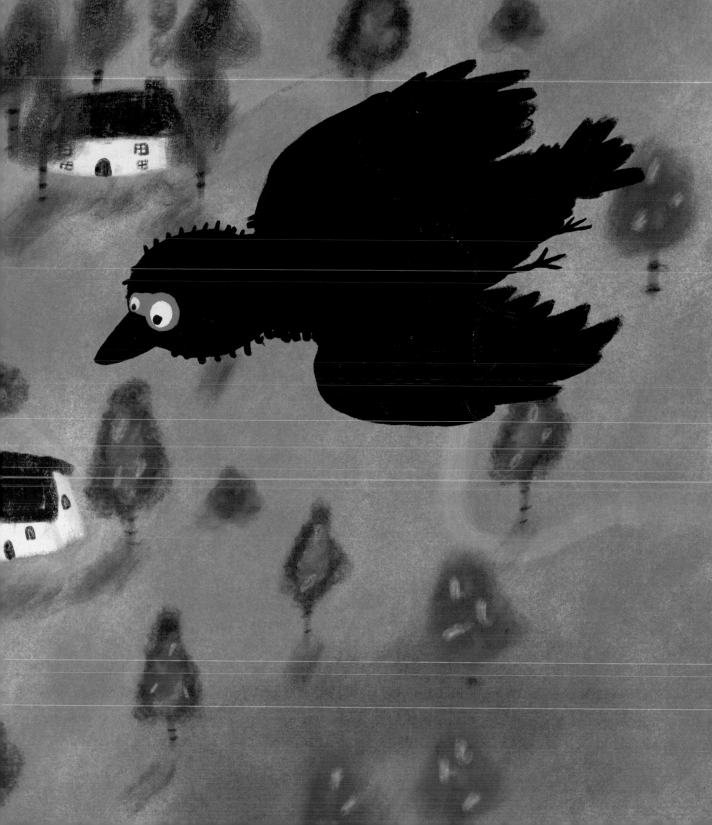

was also watching.

It **swooped** down, scaring the birds away!

Emma shouted,
"Naughty crow! Shoo, shoo!"

Each time the crow pecked
at the bird feeder,

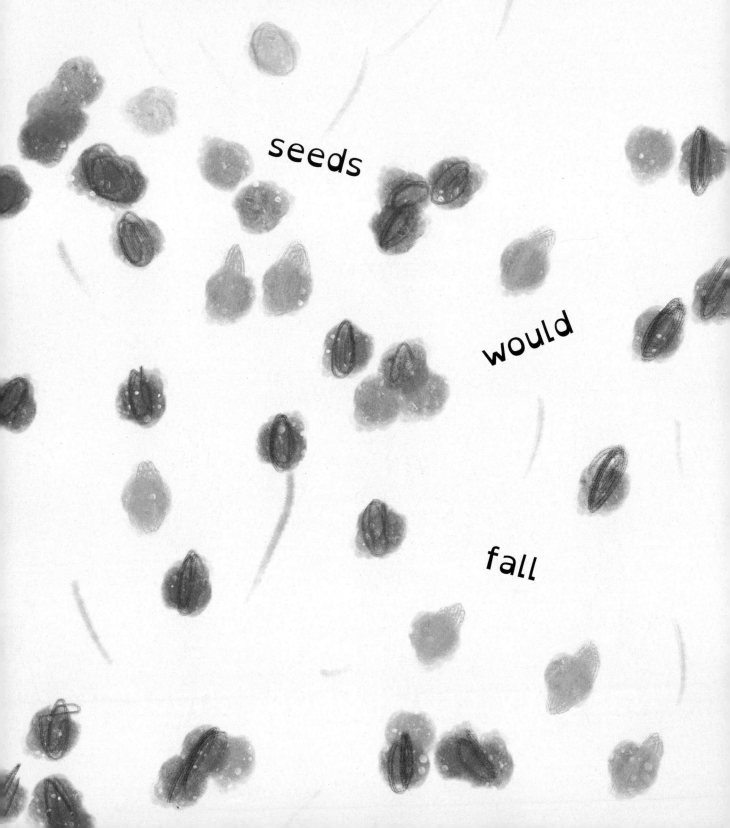

seeds

would

fall

to

the

ground

and snuggle into the soil.

The feathered family stopped coming
to the tree and could only watch
from high above, sitting on a telephone
wire like music notes upon a stave.

The crow grew

fatter

and

fatter.

Winter came, bringing festive excitement

but the greenfinches were
still nowhere to be seen.

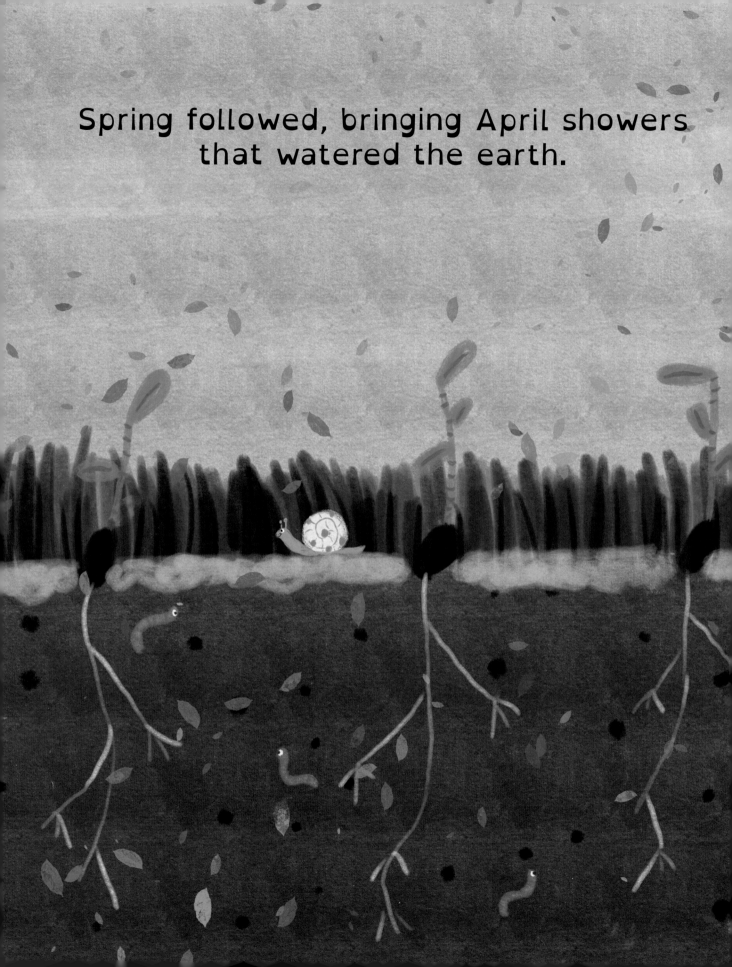

Spring followed, bringing April showers
that watered the earth.

Some of the sunflower seeds
that the crow had scattered

began   to grow.

Fluffy **white** lambs played in the fields

Baaaa!

that surrounded the cottage.

Baaaa!

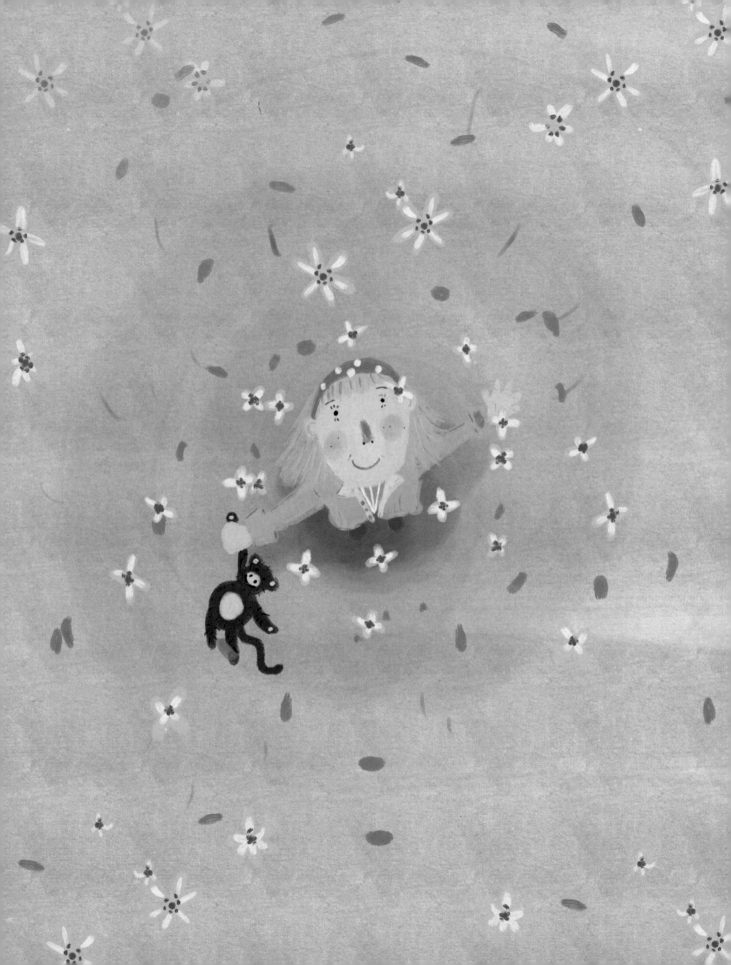

The apple blossom
looked so pretty that
Emma mistook its petals
for snowflakes swirling
to the ground.
More flowers burst
into life.

During the month of July, Emma counted

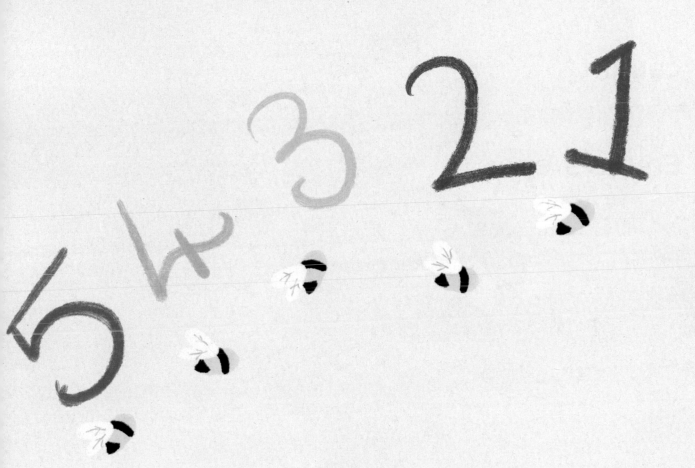

5 4 3 2 1

On the morning of

her special day,

something

caught

Emma's eye.

A beautiful

sunflower

turned

its head,

with ladybirds

forming a

smile on its face.

Emma also spotted a family of greenfinches at the bird feeder.

One of the adults had a distinctive golden feather on his tail.

It was Flash!

He had returned to feed on Emma's sunflower and made her birthday even more special.

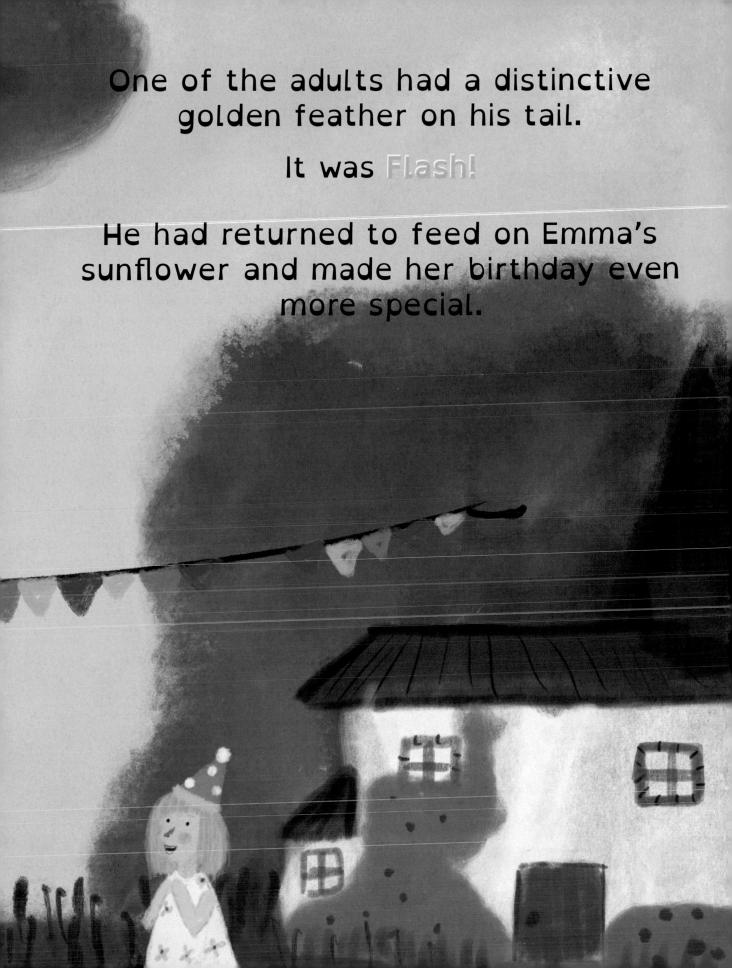

Phillipa is the creator of Rupert's Snowman, a much loved festive tale based on a true story about the time her son refused to leave his snowman behind after a snow day.

She studied Creative Short Story Writing at the Cambridge University ICE and has an MA from The Royal College of Art.

Emma's Sunflower was inspired by her daughter after she was playfully accused of favouritism towards her son!

Grace Ward, the illustrator of Emma's Sunflower and Rupert's Snowman is dyslexic and she chose a font called Open Dyslexic to tell her stories. The unique shape of each letter can help prevent confusion through flipping and swapping letters because they have a heavier bottom. The dyslexic reader will be able to quickly work out which part of the word is down and this aids in recognizing the correct letter.

"Drawing helped me to communicate when I was younger because as a dyslexic I struggled with the written word. It's important to me that the illustrations speak louder than the text so the reader gets an instant understanding of the narrative. The font I've used uses unique shapes to make it easier for the reader because the text won't jump about as much" Grace Ward, illustrator of Emma's Sunflower and Rupert's Snowman.

Can you make a face with natural objects from the garden or park? It might be tricky to get ladybirds to stay still for long enough (!) so why not use seeds, leaves, nuts, pebbles, and flowers?

Emma hopes that the greenfinch family will return after the crow has scared the birds away and she waits patiently for their return. Can you think of a time when you really wanted something and had to wait? Was it for a special day or present or did you have to wait to see a family member or friend?

What do Emma's sunflower seeds need to make them grow?

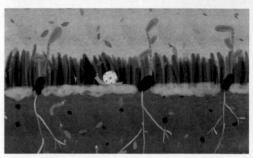

Can you spot all of the illustrations of the **crow?** (Hint: There are 10 in total.)